Chinese Tale Series

中国神话

Removing the Mountains

愚公移山

Adapted by *Feng Jiannan from an Ancient Chinese Fairy Tale*
Illustrated by *Ni Shaoyong*

据中国古代神话
冯健男　改编
倪绍勇　绘画

Dolphin Books

海豚出版社　北京

First Edition 1991

一九九一年　第一版

Hard cover: ISBN 0-8351-2731-1　ISBN 7-80051-685-7
Paperback: ISBN 0-8351-2732-X　ISBN 7-80051-686-5

Copyright 1991 by Dolphin Books, Beijing, China

Published by Dolphin Books
24 Baiwanzhuang Road, Beijing 100037, China

Distributed by China International Book Trading Corporation
21 Chegongzhuang Xilu, Beijing 100044, China
P.O. Box 399, Beijing, China

Printed in the People's Republic of China

在中华人民共和国印刷

Long, long ago, there were two high mountains, Taihang and Wangwu. The two towering mountains had a circumference of 350 kilometres.

古时侯有两座方圆七百里、高万丈的太行山和王屋山。

They obstructed the way from south to north.

这两座大山阻挡着南来北往的通道。

An old man called the Foolish Old Man lived on the northern side of the mountains. He was ninety, but very healthy and strong.

山北面住着一位老汉名叫愚公,他虽然已经九十岁啦,但身体还很强壮。

The old man was unyielding. When he wanted to do something, he would never give up until the goal was reached.

愚公有个犟脾气，他无论干什么事，不干完决不罢休。

When the Foolish Old Man and his neighbours wanted to go anywhere, they had to make a detour because beyond their doorway stood the two great peaks, Taihang and Wangwu, obstructing the way.

由于太行山、王屋山的阻挡,愚公和邻居们每次外出都要绕道而行,多走百里山路,感到很不方便。

One evening, the Foolish Old Man said to his dear ones, "Though I am ninety, I still insist on digging up the two peaks, in order to make things convenient for the later generations." His children and grandchildren all agreed to his decision.

一天晚上，愚公对全家人说："我虽已九十岁了，但是为了使后人进出方便，我们一起来挖平这两座大山吧！"儿孙们听了都一致赞成。

His wife worried about him, saying, "You are too old to do this. Besides, where shall we move the rocks and earth?"

愚公的妻子担心地说:"如今你年已古稀,凭你的精力怎么能挖平太行山和王屋山呢?再说挖出来的泥土、石块又放到哪儿去?"

Their children and grandchildren answered in one voice, "We are young. We can finish this hard work in spite of difficulties. We can throw the rocks and earth into the sea."

没等愚公开口，儿孙们便异口同声地说："爷爷老了有我们，再大的困难也不怕，挖出来的泥土、石块可以倒进海里。"

As soon as the Kitchen God heard their dialogue, he went out immediately to report all this to the Mountain God.

他们全家商谈的话全被灶王爷听到,他连夜奔上山去告诉了山神。

After the Mountain God knew this, he laughed heartily, saying, "The old man is too foolish. Don't imagine he can dig up such a big rock."

山神听后哈哈大笑说:"这个老头儿真是太愚蠢啦,我看他连山上的一块大石头也休想移动。"

Early in the morning of the following day, carrying baskets, sledgehammers and spades, the Foolish Old Man led his three children and three grandchildren to the mountains. They began their work.

　　第二天清晨，愚公便领着他的三个儿子和三个孙子挑着箩筐，扛着大锤、铁铲来到大山脚下挖起山来。

The rocks were as hard as iron. When the old man hit the sledgehammer on the rock, sparks flew off in all directions. In a short time, his hands were blistered from the hammer.

谁知这山上的石头比铁还硬，愚公一锤抡上去只见火星四溅，一会儿，他的手上便磨起血泡来。

The Foolish Old Man and his children and grandchildren worked very hard. They hit the rocks, dug earth and carried the heavy baskets. They were all wet with sweat.

愚公和他的儿孙们挥汗如雨,不停地锤呀,挖呀,挑完一筐又一筐。

In the evening, the old man and his children and grandchildren were still busy carrying baskets between the mountains and the sea.

在愚公的带领下，他们披星戴月地挑着千斤重担，有如穿梭般在山与海之间来往运行。

When they arrived home, it was dawn.

当他们回家的时候，天已东方泛白，黎明了。

The following day, they started their hard work again.

新的一天开始了，他们祖孙三代又在这样不停地挖啊，运啊。

One of their neighbours was a widow. When she saw all this,
she was deeply moved.

邻居京城氏是个寡妇。她看见愚公一家不辞辛苦地挖山筑路，十分感
动。

The widow came to the work site with her only son—a child of seven years.

她领着刚满七岁的独养儿子来到了工地上。

She said to the old man, "Old grandpa, let my child join you!"
The old man was glad to accept the young boy as a team
member.

　　她对愚公说:"老爷爷,请让我的儿子也来和你们一起挖山筑路吧!"愚
公高兴地答应了。

The old man and his dear ones were greatly encouraged by the woman's action. They worked even harder than before.

寡妇将七岁的独子送来参加移山，使愚公一家受到很大的鼓舞。他们挖得更起劲了。

When the people of the surrounding areas knew this, they expressed their admiration for him. They each tried to do something, such as sending food and water for them in order to support their work.

愚公移山的消息很快地传开啦，人们都非常敬佩他，纷纷前来送饭、送水，支援挖山。

But when his old friend, Wise Old Man, heard about this project, he said to him, "Old brother, you are old and ailing. How can you move the high mountains away? You are overestimating your strength."

愚公有一个老朋友叫智叟。他得知此事后,忙跑来劝愚公说:"老哥,像你这样风烛残年的人怎么能铲平大山呢?真有点自不量力了!"

The Foolish Old Man replied, smiling, "Nothing in the world is difficult for one who sets his mind on it. When I die, my sons and grandsons will carry on; when they die, there will be their sons and grandsons. Some day we can clear them away."

愚公笑笑说:"世上无难事,只怕有心人。我死了还有我的儿子,儿子死了还有孙子,子子孙孙是没有穷尽的。可那山挖一点少一点,总有一天能把它挖平的。"

After hearing his friend's reply, the Wise Old Man was speechless. He went away quietly.

愚公的这些话驳得智叟哑口无言,他只好悄悄地走了。

More than one year later, half of the two high mountains was moved away.

经过一年多的时间，太行山和王屋山终于被挖去了一半。

It scared the Mountain God.

这可吓坏了山神。

Standing on the top of the mountains, the Mountain God looked at them. He said to himself, "What shall I do if they go on like this?"

　　他站在山顶上仔细向下一看，只见愚公和他的子孙们正挖得起劲呢。他想：如果一直这样不停地挖下去，我可怎么办？

The Mountain God gave a puff at the work site in order to stop their work. The wind howled over the work site. The old man and his children and grandchildren could not even stand firm in the strong wind.

他为了阻止愚公移山，便向山下吹了一口长气，顿时工地上狂风大作，飞沙走石，吹得愚公和他的子孙们站也站不稳。

The old man let his children and grandchildren stand there hand in hand.

这时愚公叫孩儿们手拉手地紧紧站在一起，狂风便吹不倒他们了。

When the Mountain God found that they were not scared by the strong wind, he had a big snake attack them.

山神见狂风没能吹跑他们，又将握在手里的一条大蛇向他们放去。

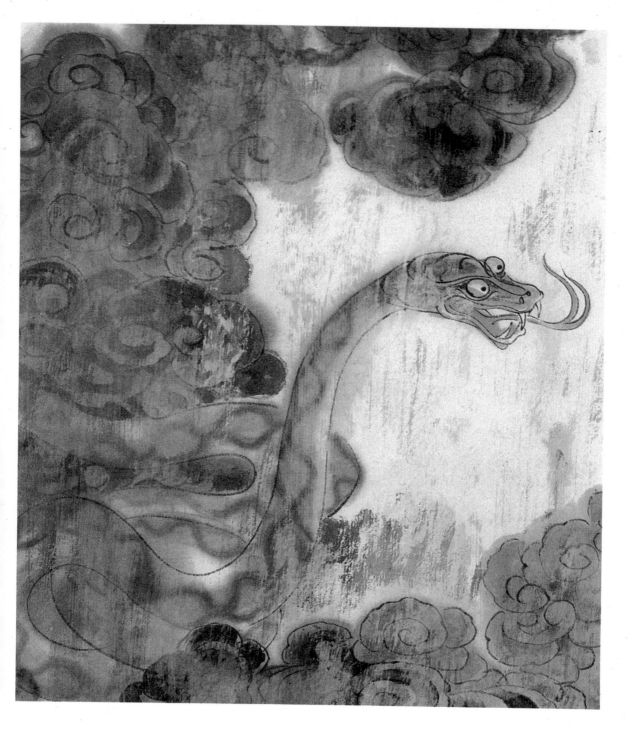

The big snake opened his large mouth and crawled quickly toward them.

那条大蛇张着嘴，很快地向愚公们窜来。

As soon as the old man saw the snake crawling toward them, he ordered his children and grandchildren to run different directions. Thus the big snake failed to hurt them.

当大蛇快窜到他们身边的时候,愚公忙叫大家各自向不同的方向闪开,大蛇便扑了个空。

They quickly came back to the work site and began to fight against the big snake. They threw rocks at it and beat it with spades and sledgehammers. The snake crawled away in panic.

说时迟，那时快，愚公叫大家拿起石头、铁铲和大锤，向大蛇打去，大蛇吓跑了。

After the Mountain God's schemes and intrigues met with defeat, he flew to the heaven to report all this to the Heavenly Emperor.

山神连施两计都失败了,便慌忙地上天将愚公移山的事情报告了天帝。

After hearing what the Mountain God told him, the Heavenly Emperor was moved by the old man's indomitable spirit.

天帝听后反而深为愚公的这种坚韧不拔的精神所感动。

The Heavenly Emperor sent down two strong gods to carry the mountains away on their backs.

于是，天帝命令两位力气最大的天神去搬走太行山和王屋山。

In the evening of that day, the two gods carried the mountains away on their backs.

当天夜里,这两位天神便将太行山和王屋山背走了。

From then on, the place became flat land. People planted crops in the fields. They always got bumper harvests. People lived a happy life, thanks to the determination of the old man.

从此，这一带便成了一片平原，连一块较高的丘陵也没有了。人们精耕细作，五谷丰收，过着安定的生活。